MS. RUBY
TAKES A
WALK
IN THE PARK

ISBN 979-8-88644-274-8 (Paperback)
ISBN 979-8-88644-275-5 (Digital)

Covenant Books
11661 Hwy 707
Murrells Inlet, SC 29576
www.covenantbooks.com

MS. RUBY TAKES A WALK IN THE PARK

Toni Gilmer

It was a sunny spring day. Oliver the kitten, Jack the puppy, and Petey the bird decided to go to the park to play. They were having so much fun. "Hey, Jack, let's race to see who is faster."

"Petey, fly up in the tree. You can be the judge to see who wins."

"I don't want to," said Petey.

"You're afraid," said Oliver and Jack. "You're not a real bird." The more they teased Petey, the sadder he became.

Ms. Ruby, an elephant, was taking a walk in the park with her son, Joey. She heard the unkind words being said. "Why don't we go over and see what is going on?" she said to Joey.

She asked all the animals to gather around, "I have a story to tell you. It is the same story my grandma told me when I was young."

She began to say to them that making fun of someone is not kind. Oliver, Jack, Petey, and Joey all listened quietly. Words we say can help or hurt someone. She told them that instead of making fun of Petey, they should say kind words. Petey told them how he had fallen out of the nest and was injured when he was very young.

"Oh my," said Ms. Ruby. Making fun of Petey made him feel bad. "There is a way to help Petey and make him feel better.

Why don't you try saying kind words?" said Ms. Ruby. "You might even help Petey fly again." Oliver and Jack and Joey agreed.

"Petey, you can do it. You're strong now. We know you can fly high, Petey," they all said. "We are here to catch you if you start to fall." They continued yelling, "You can do it, Petey!"

21

All of a sudden, Petey took off and flew high up in the tree! He was so happy that he began to fly all over the sky above them and started singing.

Ms. Ruby told Oliver and Jack and Joey that using kind words is always better than unkind words, "See how happy your kind words have made Petey!"

Oliver and Jack told Petey that they were sorry for making fun of him. They learned an important lesson about words that day.

Oliver, Jack, Petey, and Joey played in the park the rest of the day. They all had a great day filled with fun!

About the Author

Our words are powerful. The author's goal is to help young readers learn the importance of the words we speak.

CPSIA information can be obtained
at www.ICGtesting.com
Printed in the USA
JSHW060715171122
33346JS00004B/42

9 798886 442748